MY FAVORITE TEACHER

Tammy S. Dalley

Contents

CHAPTER 1: One Hot Customer!!

DAISY

Just a few more months, I keep telling myself.

A few more months and I will be leaving this shitty place and forever be able to get away from my mother and her disgusting boyfriend.

My dad was killed in an accident at work and the day I found out I lost him, was the same day I felt I had lost my best friend.

When I was little, I had a lot of friends and things were great. But then after he left everyone around me started treating me like shit and calling me names and had even made fun of my dad's death.

I was really close to my dad and miss him every single day.

After my dad died, my mom spiraled out of 'control' I'd like to call it as she turned to drinking which caused me to always have to take care of her.

Then when I was ten years old, my mom brought home a guy named Roger who happens to now be my stepdad and treats me no different than she does. Luckily I'm curvy and unattractive cause that way I don't have to worry about him touching me inappropriately. Or at least that's what he's told me.

Neither one of them were up today so I was able to leave for work without having to see them.

I work at a place that sells everything you would ever need for your home. Which I liked cause when I finally get my own place, I plan to get several things from here using my employee discount.

After putting my things in the employee break room, I headed out to my cash register and prepared for my shift.

Throughout the day, everything was not too bad.

Then a guy came walking in who looked to be in his early to mid twenties with tattoos covering him head to toe and slicked back hair. He looked like your typical badass, built and sexy as hell.

My co-worker and best friend Janet, had just come back from break.

"Hey gorgeous!" She says as she does all the time.

"Hey." I tell her.

I am always excited to see her. She is almost eighteen as well, has awesome parents who like me a whole lot and who always has had my back since the eighth grade. She is very blunt, has long brown hair, gorgeous green eyes, is curvy and just the most greatest person you could ever know.

"So how is your day going so far?" She asks.

"It's going." I reply with a chuckle.

"So I noticed you checking out the hot customer over there." She smiles and winks at me.

"Yeah." I say shyly while blushing.

"You know, you should really go and talk to him."

"Yeah, no." I tell her.

"Oh come on, why not? And don't you dare give me that bullshit that it's because you are curvy, fat, ugly or whatever bullshit things you say about yourself that are far from the truth." She tells me.

"You know me, I get real nervous around guys like him." I asked.

"Believe it or not, a lot of fit men like curvy girls and besides, if he isn't interested in you in a sexual way or even as a friend, than it's his loss." She says.

I look at her for a brief moment.

"I don't know." I reply.

"Fine. Then I will go give him your number and tell him how hard you want him to fuc....." She began before I stopped her.

"Fine. I'll talk to him just, please stop saying things like that." I chuckled a little bit before making my way towards the hottest guy I have ever seen.

I take in a few deep breaths and walk up to him as I see he's checking out some beds.

"Hi. Can I help you with anything?" I asked.

He turns turns his head and looks at me and smiles.

"Yeah. Uh, I'm looking for a good mattress and some bedding to go with a California King sized bed." He says.

"Okay. Well, our California King Sized beds are towards the back over there." I say as I point to the back left. "And there you'll find a few with mattresses on them along with some other bedding items you need." I tell him nervously.

"Could you show me?" He asks.

"Sure. Right this way." I tell him and I turn and start walking towards the back as he walks beside me and my god does he smell so damn good.

"So how long you worked here?" He asks.

Wow, he's very confident. I'm so jealous.

"Two years." I reply.

"Do you like it?" He asks.

"It's nice. Plus the discounts are awesome." I tell him.

"That's always a plus." He laughs. Which his laugh is so sexy.

We get to the few selections of the beds and I show him the one that's my favorite. "So, I'm not sure what type you're looking for but this one is nice. I like cherry wood. I think it's a really good one for as far as looks go and it's just nice." I hurry and finish as I begin getting more nervous I'm starting to have trouble thinking of what to say.

"I'll take it then." He smiles.

"Okay." I reply as I take put my IPAD they give us all to place in the orders. "When would you like it delivered?" I asked.

"Tomorrow." He smiles.

"Okay. Now, for the other items. Such as bedding's and everything, they're over here." I began to say.

"Wait, can I test out the mattress? You did say we can do that right?" He asks.

"Of course. Go ahead." I tell him.

"Would you lay on it with me?" He asks.

"Um..." I began to think of something to say really quick.

"It's just, I wanted to see what it would be like with someone lying next to me." He says.

"Oh, okay." I replied and went to lay down next to him on the bed. Which he probably wants to see if his girlfriend would be able to be there with him.

We lay there for a couple of minutes until I get more nervous although not until I start thinking about what it might be like of he made out with me and we fell asleep in each other's arms after making love.

"That sounds really nice." I hear him chuckle and immediately I sit up and know that my face has got to be as red as a tomato from the embarrassment I feel.

"I-I'm sorry. I didn't mean to say that out loud. Just come to the register when you're done and Janet will ring you up. Thank you for coming to our store and have a great day." I hurry up and say to him as I walk as quickly as I could to Janet to have her ring him up when he was ready.

I have never felt so humiliated in my entire life. And now it happened to be in front of a hot guy? Oh my god, this sucks so much.

CHAPTER 2: Feeling Like A Damn Teenager

ASHTON

I really hated shopping but I just moved here and was gonna start teaching at a high school the day after tomorrow and still didn't have any furniture and some things. So I found a home items type of a place and decided I needed to get stuff today.

When I got there it was huge. I quickly read the signs and started going down to the aisles I needed to but first, I needed to head upstairs and look at the beds and everything.

As I got upstairs and began to look at a few lamps and everything, the most beautiful girl asked me if I needed anything.

She was curvy and had to be between the ages of 18-20. Which would be awesome cause I'm 24. She was a little bit shy I could tell but her hazel green eyes, oh my god, I could look into those all day long. And her lips and whole curvy body, oh my.

She ended up showing me the beds and what I needed.

While looking at the beds, I laid down and asked her to join me. Although I wanted to do nothing more but to take her right then and there, not caring if rather or not anybody saw us.

Then as she laid down beside me, she said out loud what she wished I would do to her and I would do it. But instead, I comment on it and she turns bright red and runs off.

I didn't mean to scare her off. Shit. Oh well, I guess I can always look for her next time or when I check out.

However, during check out, it was Janet that checked me out and as she gave me my receipt, I was looking for the girl that helped me, but she was nowhere to be found. So I just left and wished Janet a great rest of her day.

When I got home, I continued on unpacking the several boxes I had and after I was done, I took a shower, ate some dinner, had a few beers and went to bed.

Before falling asleep, I couldn't help but think of that girl I met today who helped me at the store. Maybe I'll go back there soon and hopefully see her there again. And this time, get her name.

****

Monday came real fast and I was all unpacked and had decided that I would arrive to school before all the kids started to arrive.

I said 'hi' to several of the teachers in the faculty lounge and then headed towards my classroom.

I was a little bit nervous, seeing as to how this was my second job teaching and I just recently replaced a teacher in which to me, I personally feel a little awkward and know there might be tension.

So after setting up and sitting down at my desk, waiting for the students, I finally heard the first bell out of two.

Within a minute, students began pouring into the classroom, talking about their weekend and everything.

Of course, all the girls were drooling and fixing themselves a little bit once they saw me which always baffled me to be honest.

Then once the second bell rang, I began to take a look at the list of names I had for attendance and was about to get started by introducing myself when the door opens and in walks the girl that I have been thinking about since a couple days ago.

This is great. She is in my class. I'll be able to see her everyday. Quickly I felt myself start to smile.

"Good morning." I greeted her and she didn't make any eye contact with me.

"Sorry I'm late." She says as she continues to look down at the floor.

"That's okay. It happens." I reply.

She then looks up at me and looks horrified and shocked. Was I really that hideous? She then starts heading to the back of the class towards her desk.

Shit! I thought. I freaked her out that bad yesterday and now she can't even make eye contact with her. She must think I'm a creep.

I shake the thoughts out of my head as I continue.

"Good morning class. My name is Ashton Moon but you all can call me Mr. Moon. I'll be your new teacher this year and I'll have you all continue off on the same assignment your old teacher, Mr. Rooney, had you guys working on before he left." I finished. "If you have any questions or anything, feel free to ask away."

A girl raises her hand who looks to be the slut of the classroom.

"Mr. Moon?" She asks while raising her hand.

"Yes Vicki?" I asked.

"Is it true that you're single?" She asks.

"That's a personal question. However, yes, I'm single." I replied to her while looking in the back at the girl, who I found out her name was Daisy.

I then take a seat in my chair behind the desk and throughout the rest of the period, I look up information through the school records about her and most of the time keep looking at her while she always was reading the book for the assignment they were given.

She seemed sad today and I wondered what was going on.

However, I was afraid that I might upset her or freak her out a bit. So maybe I should just wait until it's not the first day or week.

What the hell is wrong with me? Why is she making me nervous as though I'm a teenager or something?

Well, this year is gonna be very interesting.

CHAPTER 3: Too Distracted?

DAISY

I can't believe that the universe hates me that much to where the hot guy I helped and humiliated myself in front of the other day, he was gonna be my teacher for the rest of my Senior year. I swear, I just want to hide in a hole right now.

I notice out the corner of my eye every so often that he is looking at me a lot throughout most of the class but I ignore his looks. I can't look at him after what happened the other day.

As soon as the bell rang, I left as quickly as possible and put my notebook that had my intimate thoughts and some of my steamy love stories I wrote, into my backpack and left as quickly as possible.

Once I got out into the hallway, I felt like I could finally breathe. I heard Janet come up from behind me.

"Hey girl, what's up?" She asks me. "Where were you this morning?"

"Oh, I'm sorry. I just had a bad morning." I tell her.

Of course it's a lie cause this morning, I slept through my alarm clock by accident cause of having to stay up late last night to try and heal myself from the beatings I got from Roger. I can't tell Janet the truth cause I know she would kill him.

"Okay...." she replies not sounding completely convinced. "Well then tell me how Mr. Rooney's boring class was." She laughs.

"Actually, Mr. Rooney retired I guess. We have a new teacher now." I tell her while we start walking to our next class.

"Oh really? Is it another old and boring man?" She teases.

"No. Actually, he's....in his early twenties I think." I tell her.

"Oooo. Is he hot?" She asks.

"Well, yeah. Actually, remember that guy the other day who you told me to talk to at work?" I asked her.

"Yeah." She says.

"He's my teacher." I tell her.

"No fucking way! The hottie with a body is your teacher? Oh my god, I'm jealous that you get to stare at him all day. You are so lucky." She says.

"Shut up. It isn't like that." I tell her while we both share a laugh together and then split off to our next classes.

Throughout the rest of the day, I was glad that I only had one class with Ashton, I mean Mr. Moon. That is, until Janet reminds me that for my last period of the day, I had to go back into Mr. Moon's classroom cause I was his Mr. Rooney's teacher's assistant when she texted me telling me that at least my last period will be more fun and then sent a wink emoji face to me.

As soon as I got to the door, I took in a couple of deep breaths and opened the door and saw Mr. Moon sitting behind his desk, looking through his computer when he turns his head over to look at me after he hears the door.

"Daisy?!" He says while sitting up abruptly. "What can I do for you?" He says while looking a bit nervous.

"I was Mr. Rooney's teacher's assistant. So is there anything you need help with?" I ask him.

"Uh....Yeah. actually, may I have you please give me a hand with unpacking and organizing some supplies in those boxes in the back there and organizing them in those cabinets back there?" He asks.

"Sure." I say while setting down my bag on one of the desks as I begin walking towards the back and start to unpack and organize the cabinets.

I felt like most of the time like I was being watched.

I had caught him out the corner of my eye, looking at me when he was supposed to be grading papers.

Technically just a few minutes were left but when I looked at my phone, I saw a message from my mom telling me she needed me home right away. Then as I tried to look at Mr. Moon and ask if I could leave, I noticed he was really focused on the papers he was grading at the moment so I just grabbed my backpack and started making my way to the door.

"I will finish the rest tomorrow Mr. Moon." I tell him before leaving.

He didn't look up at me. Was he upset with me? I hope not. Then again, it wouldn't be a surprise. I've gotten in trouble before for just breathing the same air as my mom. I don't know, it was something as stupid as that.

CHAPTER 4: Will There Be Anything Else?

ASHTON

After I ask her to put away and organize a few things in the back cabinets, I try and continue to grade the papers. However, I can't seem to focus on them when she's standing there with those sexy curves that makes me wanna just grab onto her hips and....I stop myself and shake those kinds of thoughts out of my head.

I don't know why I thought about those things. She is my student and it is illegal.

I'm not sure what made me feel so drawn and also attracted to her. I want to know everything about her though.

I especially want to at least apologize to her for freaking her out the other day. I didn't mean to.

The bell rings to indicate last period for the day is over.

"I'll finish the rest tomorrow Mr. Moon." I hear her say to me while on her way out and before I could say thank you even, she was already gone.

I've been thinking all day long about how great this was that I would be able to get to see her. However, now, I'm thinking it might not be such a good thing, seeing the effect she has on me.

This might become harder than I thought. I could lose my license and all my credibility that I have worked so hard for.

There must be a way that I can not make it as obvious how I feel about her.

So starting today, I did just that. After grading papers from the project their old teacher had them doing before he left, as soon as everyone took their seat to begin class, I used that time to address them about how they all did.

I grabbed the papers and handed them to the student sitting in the front row to pass them back to the others.

"Some of you did really good, some better than others. Then there were some of you who CLEARLY didn't even try. Which I will not tolerate. If you fail my class, I want it to be because you at least tried. I don't want any of you to give up. If you have any questions, then you can ask me after class or after school, but my grades are all final." I tell them.

For the rest of the period, I began going over their homework for the rest of the week and couldn't help myself from looking every now and then over at Daisy who I can tell is taking notes but seems to look really upset. Most likely cause I gave her a 'D-'

So as soon as the bell rang and everyone got up and began leaving to get to their next class, I see Daisy walking up to my desk slowly and then stops in front of me.

"Mr. Moon?" She asks.

"Yes, Daisy?" I replied.

"Why did you give me a D-?" She asks me with a scared and worried look on her face.

"Because, you didn't explain in detail how that one family survived under those horrific circumstances back in that era." I tell her, which is the truth.

"But I did. On the 3rd page, I explained in full detail what all they had to do and even provided more details, if anything, on their story and how they survived." She begins to argue.

"Well, I'm sorry, but all grades are final." I tell her with a smirk.

"Do you really hate me that much? Or is this just cause you're one of THOSE teachers who makes it impossible to pass their class because of some personal issue?!" She fires back at me and to be honest, I'm taken back yet impressed at the same time to how she just responded.

"I'll see you after class. We'll discuss it then." I tell her and then turn my chair to face my computer and begin to answer a couple of my EMAIL's with my back turned towards her while I next hear her leaving and slamming the door shut.

The fact that she had called me out the way she did, definitely didn't help me in how I feel about her.

Throughout the day, I was actually worried that maybe she might not even show up after school. Then I see the door opening up and she walks inside.

She sets down her bag and seems to look a little bit more calm than she was this morning.

"I'm sorry about this morning in how I reacted. I shouldn't have talked to you like that." She apologizes.

"It's okay. You have every right to be upset." I tell her. "But, I wasn't trying to be hard on you. You're assignment was to do an essay about a specific topic but you fell short of the amount of words you were supposed to write and you also had several grammar issues. Some of the sentences didn't even make any sense to be honest." I tell her.

"I understand. But is there anything I can do to bring my grade up?" She asks me.

"I'll get back to you once I figured out an assignment you could do." I tell her.

"Okay." She replies.

"For now, however, I need for you to go and finish putting the last of the supplies in the boxes into the cabinets in the back." I tell her.

"Alright." She replies and walks to the back and begins to put the last of the supplies into the cabinets. Then she walks back up to me. "What else would you like me to do?" She asks me.

There were a few things I wanted her to do but that weren't appropriate. Damnit, what the hell is wrong with me?

"No." I tell her. "Actually, you can leave. I will see you tomorrow." I tell her.

"Okay." She smiles while grabbing her bag and then heading out.

CHAPTER 5: What Did I Do?!

DAISY

I'm not sure what Mr. Moon's problem was but I think he really does hate me with a passion and that is why he was giving me a hard time with my paper.

Oh well, doesn't matter now. I needed to hurry and get ready to leave for work soon so right as I got home, I ran upstairs to take a quick shower and get ready for work when as soon as I came out of the shower with only a towel wrapped around me, I suddenly got pushed hard up against the wall in my bedroom with a hand covering my mouth immediately.

"Don't say anything, you fucking bitch!" Roger warns me. He then starts looking me up and down while the strong odor of whiskey is being breathed onto me from his mouth as he moves in closer, causing me to cry and to try to struggle free from his grasp.

"I said don't fucking make a noise or move! We can do this the easy way or the hard way. I know how much you have been wanting me. And since your mother isn't home..." He says with his lips closer to my neck.

I start crying louder and the next thing I hear is my mom walking in through the front door downstairs and calling out to us.

"Are you guys home?! I have some great news!" We hear her say.

"We'll be right down." He yells down at her before looking back at me. "Don't say a word you fat ugly whore! Cause she won't believe you anyways." He tells me, which obviously isn't true and is making me want to throw up.

He next hits me hard in the eye making me know right away that it's gonna close shut and then to make things worse as I'm on the floor and holding my eye, he kicks me hard in the stomach and I begin to throw up along with feeling so much pain, I can't speak or even move.

So I just lay there on the floor for a few more moments before finally having the strength to be able to reach my phone in my purse that's on the floor by my bed to where I text Janet to let her know I can't come in and will be not going into school for the rest of the week cause I was sick with a stomach virus.

Now of course she knows the truth in what really happened because I have used the same excuse before. darkness is the next thing that consumes me and I end up blacking out there on the floor.

****

Two Weeks Later.....

I haven't gone to school in two weeks which was a week more than I had planned.

However, I am coming back today and thanks to Janet grabbing my homework from all my classes everyday I missed, including Mr. Moon's, I am not behind in my work or anything of that sort.

Turns out too that for the next couple of months, my mom and Roger were gonna be out of the country on some sort of business trip for my mom's work. Which don't ask me how she has a good job like that when she drinks a lot. I still haven't figured that one out yet myself.

When I walked into Mr. Moons' class, I had tried to avoid eye contact with him as I had my hair covering my face as much as possible as the fact that my bruises haven't entirely disappeared and I just ran out of concealer.

I could tell that even though I wasn't looking at him, he was staring at me.

I thought I'd be able to go right past him if once the bell rang but no such luck.

"Ms. Conrad. I'd like to speak with you for a moment." I hear him say.

I close my eyes and flinch a little bit as he calls me what people call my mom and then start to turn around and walk up to his desk.

"Is everything alright?" He asks.

"Of course." I reply while still avoiding eye contact.

"I heard you were sick with a stomach virus." He tells me although the look on his face shows me that he doesn't believe me for one second that that was why I wasn't here.

"Yeah but I'm a lot better now." I assure him.

"Okay." He says letting out a breath. "Well, if you ever need to talk, I'm here." He smiles at me.

"Thanks." I reply and turn to leave and head to my next class before I'm late.

It's not that I don't believe Mr. Moon isn't genuinely expressing concern about my well being or anything but I can't involve anyone and definitely can't go to the police and I know if I told the Principal or a teacher about what's going on, I know that by law they have to say something. That's why I have always tried coming up with a convincing excuse whenever they saw bruises or something on me.

I swear that sometimes or I should say most times, I think about killing myself. I keep thinking about how much the world would be better off without me here. Sure Janet would miss me and be heart broken but it's not like hundreds or even ten people would show up to my funeral who truly really ever cared as much as Janet does.

Some say that we were different things in other lifetimes before. However, if that's really true, then what the hell did I do to come back into this kind of a life?

CHAPTER 6: The Ride Home

ASHTON

My god I have missed Daisy. When Janet told me that she was out cause she had a stomach virus, something deep inside was telling me she wasn't sick. In fact, I have seen the same demeanor that she shows, in another girl I used to know years ago who was abused and tried to hide it all the time. It was my little sister.

It was none of my business and if it was what I believed it was then it was my legal duty to say something and report it to the right authorities. Although I wouldn't do that seeing as to how I've seen how they try to 'help' out.

I tried not to give her a look of pity but I couldn't help it as I saw her hair covering most of her face as she looked down and sat down at her desk and wasn't making any eye contact with me at all for the rest of the class.

Then before she left to go towards her next class, I asked her if she was alright and just in the same tone and same excuse as my sister had told me before after her boyfriend had just got done beating her. She said 'yes'.

I really meant it when I also told her she could talk to me anytime about whatever, which is the same as what I told all the students.

She gave me a weak smile but still, I accepted it the same.

Finally after school was over, I stayed back to grade some papers before heading home.

While getting into my car, I had thought about Daisy. Although that's all the time practically that I do that.

So I decided to head over towards where she worked at and see if she needed a ride home from work, seeing as to how late it is and it was close to closing time for the store.

As soon as ai pulled up in front, I waited in my car while listening to music until I saw her walking out and talking with some guy instead of Janet, who I thought she'd be talking with.

I white knuckled the steering wheel as I got pissed off that she was talking to some little shit who is most likely trying to get in her pants. Doesn't he know how fragile she is?

Wait, what the hell am I saying? I shake the thoughts out of my head and then get out and start walking up towards them.

"Hey." I say.

The guy turned his head and gave me a scowl kind of like I was cock blocking him. Then I turned and saw her giving me a look of surprise and shock.

"M-Mr. Moon. What are you doing here?" She asks a little nervously while trying to hide her blush.

"I came to give you a ride. Don't you remember?" I asked her.

Before she replies, I glare at the punk kid in front of me and he starts to back off.

"I'll see ya later D." He says to her and gives her a quick kiss on the cheek while smiling at me like he knew he got me and walked away.

However, I didn't get mad. I calmed down real quick before looking back at Daisy.

"Come on, i'll take you home." I tell her as we begin walking towards my car.

She nods and walks beside me as I open up the passenger door to help her inside, then after she gets in, I close the door and get in and start to drive after she tells me where she lives.

Yes I already know from the school records where she lives however, I didn't want to sound like a creep or anything.

I couldn't stop playing the image I had just seen a minute ago with that guy touching her and kissing the side of her cheek. She probably didn't want to be rude in telling him to stop. Either way, that wasn't going to happen again.

"Who was that guy?" I asked while trying to hide my jealousy.

"Nicholas? He's just a friend I work with." She replies.

"Sure he's not your boyfriend or anything?" I asked.

"No. He's leaving tomorrow for college and besides, he's gay." I hear her say.

"Oh.." I reply with a lot of relief. "That's cool. Good for him." I tell her.

"What made you think he was my boyfriend?" She asks.

"I just thought the way you guys were talking and the body langua ge..." I stop as she chuckles a little bit.

"Yeah, right. Someone like ME have a boyfriend. That's hilarious." She tells me and my heart breaks a little bit.

"Why is it?" I ask.

"Nothing. My house is right there. With the lit up driveway." She points.

As soon as I pull up to the front of her house, I hear her start to thank me for the ride.

"You're welcome. If you ever need one to school, work, anywhere, don't hesitate to ask." I assure her with a smile.

"Thank you." She smiles in return. "Goodnight Mr. Moon." She tells me as she gets out and shuts the door and starts walking up to the front door.

I wait until she is inside the house before I drive off and head home.

Damn, how could she not see her beauty and her worth? Of course she could have a boyfriend. I think she'd be a great girlfriend. She's seventeen almost eighteen and she is curvy and beautiful.

Someone needs to help show her just how much she's worth it.

CHAPTER 7: Why So Nervous?

DAISY

I was surprised that Mr. Moon had come and picked me up to take me home after work.

However, I was even more surprised when I heard him sound jealous when asking about Nicholas, my friend and co-worker, about if we were dating.

He looked and smelled amazing. His car was beautiful and before going to bed tonight, I began thinking that maybe he wasn't jealous after all and I just misunderstood.

I mean come on, really, it's stupid to think he would be jealous. He's my teacher, of course he doesn't like me like that. I'm so dumb sometimes. I laugh to myself before falling asleep.

****

It was finally Friday although everyday has been like a Friday with me ever since my parents left.

Janet was going out of town this weekend to visit her grandparents, so that meant I was gonna be alone. Which was no big deal cause I liked hanging around the house and watch movies while eating whatever I want and relaxing.

School wasn't so bad, long, but not bad. After saying 'bye' to Janet, I walked to the grocery store before heading home and enjoying my 'binge' weekend. Or maybe I shouldn't say binged per say, cause I'm not gonna buy out the whole grocery store or anything, just gonna not worry about closet eating.

It might sound silly and weird but I felt a sense of relief when I walked inside the store knowing I could get whatever I wanted and not be worried about being judged. I don't binge everyday or every weekend, but I feel I should celebrate.

So I grabbed the cart and began heading down the candy aisle first to grab a few Junior Mints, Peanut M&M's along with a few other ones before heading to the chips aisle, soda and even granola bars. But not the fat free ones this time. Oh and can't forget a 4 pack of Magnum ice cream bars, double caramel. Mmmmm.

While trying to look for the ice cream bars, I hear a familiar sexy deep husky voice.

"Daisy?" Mr. Moon says.

"Oh, hi Mr. Moon." I reply while feeling embarrassed as I notice him looking at all the food I got. He must be thinking I'm a huge cow.

"Please, call me Ashton outside of school. Mr. Moon sounds weird and makes me feel old when I'm only twenty-four." He chuckles.

"Okay." I reply.

"You having a party?" He asks.

"Uhm...Yeah." I lied.

"Nice." He says.

We both share an awkward brief moment of silence.

"Well, have a good weekend." I tell him as I leave to get in line to check out.

When finally getting to the front and the lady starts scanning the items, I don't know why but I right away defend myself and blurt out, "I'm having a party." I smile.

She looks at me with a raised eyebrow that made me think she knew otherwise.

I felt eyes burning a hole in the back of my head but tried to ignore it and to start calming myself in my mind so that I wouldn't get anxiety.

Then finally, I paid the lady, grabbed the bags and began to leave as fast as ai could.

Then right as I began walking the couple of miles towards my house (pray for me to make it there without dying), I heard someone from my left side call out my name. I knew who that voice was.

"You need a ride?" I heard Ashton call out.

"No, it's okay. Thanks though." I reply as I continue walking.

Then I hear the car stop and see him get out and grab my bags then opens up the passenger door.

"Please, I insist. It's hot as hell out here." He suggests.

"Okay." I answer after I think about how much he's right. Plus I don't want to create a scene by grabbing my bags from his hand when there's people already looking at us.

So after getting in and buckled up and once he places the groceries in the trunk, he gets in and starts to drive towards my house.

"So what kind of a party you having?" He breaks the silence.

I am quiet for a moment as I feel bad that I lied to him. I'm not a liar. I don't want him to think that neither.

"Actually, I lied. I'm not having a party. I just told you that cause I didn't want you to think I was a fat cow that eats like this all the time." I confess and look out the window as I feel extremely embarrassed that I just said all of that.

My god, why does he make me so nervous whenever I'm around him? He's hot yes, but still, I can't be thinking this way over someone that

I have NO chance with ever. Even after I turn eighteen and even if he wasn't my teacher.

We pull up in front of the house and after thanking him for the ride, I feel him place his hand on my wrist to stop me from getting out.

"Wait, let me help you." He smiles at me before getting out and heading towards the trunk to grab my grocery bags and his?

We walk up to my house and after walking inside, he sets the groceries down amd as I start thanking him and before asking him to leave, I notice he's putting things away.

"You don't have to do that. I can do it. You should probably leave." I tell him.

He stops and lets out a breath. Oh shit, did I frustrate him? Is he gonna hit me?

He turns around and he walks out of the kitchen towards me on the other side of the counter as I back up until I hit the door behind me.

"Do you really want me to leave?" He asks as he looks down at my lips.

Shit, why does he make me so nervous?

CHAPTER 8: Just A Kiss?!?

ASHTON

Shit, I really fucked up and feel like shit when after she told me in the car that she wasn't having a party and was afraid I would think she was a cow. When the truth is, I haven't had junk food in so long, her cart looked better than mine.

Then just now, as she told me I didn't have to put away her groceries, I had stopped and let out a breath of frustration, mostly with myself for not being able to want to leave.

So as I am looking down at her lips right now, I can't stop but think about how they would feel on mine and what they would taste like.

After asking her if she wanted me to really leave, although I knew she didn't, I leaned in closer as I could see the affect I was having on her.

"N-no." She says.

"Good. Now why don't you go and pick out a movie while I order us some food and finish putting these groceries away." I tell her while being less than an inch away from her lips.

"Okay." She replies.

"Good." I tell her with a smile before pushing myself off the wall from her and heading back into the kitchen.

She heads into the living room and I can't help but check her out while imagining tracing every curve of her body from head to toe gently with my fingertips.

"What sounds good?" I called from the kitchen.

"I don't care. You pick." She calls back.

"How about some steak?" I suggest.

"Sure. Just grab some cash from my purse." She says.

"I got it." I call back to her.

Then after ordering, I see she has finally picked out a movie and so I grab us a couple glasses with ice and pour her and I some soda and walk over towards her on the couch and hand her her drink.

"Oh, thanks." She says as she takes it and takes a sip from it before setting it down on the coffee table in front of us.

"So what movie are we watching?" I asked her as I took a drink out of my glass and had my first soda in ten years. Mmmm the flavorful carbonation going down my throat tasted and felt so good.

"I don't know about you but, one of my favorite movies that I haven't seen in a long time is Jaws." She says with a hint of excitement in her voice.

"Man, that's a great classic. I haven't seen it since I was a kid. It definitely kept me from going into the water for a long time." I chuckle.

"Yeah, me too." She laughs a little bit. In which I love her laugh.

Before starting the movie, she goes upstairs to get into something more comfortable while I wait for the food.

Which it was perfect timing as I set up the food and everything and got things all ready right about the same time she came walking down.

"I hope you don't mind, I got us some plates." I tell her, not realizing how stupid that was to say.

"Of course I don't mind. That's what they're there for." She chuckles.

She takes a seat back next to me and then we started the movie and eating.

When we were done eating and while watching the movie, I felt like putting my arm around her or holding her hand but I didn't.

So mostly we were both sitting there watching the movie with an awkwardness in the air.

Then after the movie was over, we sat there for a brief moment until she got up, threw away the trash and headed towards the sink to wash the few dishes in there.

While she did that, I don't know what made me get so brave to walk up behind her while she was washing the few dishes and start to push her hair aside, exposing the side of her neck as I began moving my lips closer to her neck.

"Mr. Moon?" I hear her ask while then noticing her bite her lower lip nervously.

"I thought I told you to call me Ashton outside of school." I lowly say in her ear while placing one of my hands on the side of her waist.

"Ashton..." She says in a small moan breathless.

"You have no idea what you do to me Daisy." I tell her as I gently start placing kisses on her neck.

"What..do I do?" I hear her say breathlessly.

"You drive me crazy. You make me think things I shouldn't be because you are my student." I reply as I place another gentle kiss on her neck.

"Mmmm." I hear her let out a moan.

I begin moving my hands down her sides and then turn her around to face me, causing her to gasp.

We look into each other's eyes for a moment and as I start leaning my lips closer towards hers until I gently put mine on hers and we begin sharing a long and passionate kiss.

I lick her bottom lip for access into her mouth, that she allows.

Then as we pull our heads back a little bit to take a breath, for a moment I think maybe she regrets the kiss.

"I'm sorry." I begin.

"Don't be. I'm sorry. I just haven't kissed many, so I apologize if it was bad." She says shyly.

"You are a great kisser and have amazingly soft sweet lips." I tell her.

"Thank you. You are too." She smiles back at me.

"Thanks." I reply.

"So what now?" She asks.

"Well, I don't want to force you into doing something you don't want to do. I personally would love nothing more to be with you but, you know the risks and what could happen. So I'm gonna leave the choice up to you." I tell her. Although deep down I'm dying inside, worried she'll say 'no'.

"I do turn eighteen soon. And I can keep a secret if you can." She says with a smile.

"You have no idea how happy you just made me." I smile at her and give her another kiss.

CHAPTER 9: Either Way, I Love It

DAISY

I can't believe that I just agreed to being in a relationship with my teacher and a hot one at that. This has to be a dream.

"Where's your nearest restroom?" He asks me.

"Uh, it's the first door on the left, right around the corner." I tell him.

"Okay. I'll be right back beautiful. Pick out another movie." He smiles and gives me a kiss before walking away while I feel myself blushing.

I have the biggest smile on my face until I hear an all too familiar ringtone, my mom's cell.

"Hello?" I answered quietly while looking to make sure Ashton didn't come out.

"Finally you answer! What the hell have you been doing?!" She angrily snaps at me.

"Sorry mom. I was watching a movie." I tell her.

"Don't lie to me you fat whore! Who's there?" She snaps again at me.

"N-Nobody. I promise." I start telling her but she cuts me off.

"Better not be or else you'll be punished when we return next month." She says.

"Next month? But I thought you were coming home in two months?!" I asked suddenly feeling scared and sick.

"Well we aren't. I will be done with this whole project here in a month. So you better make sure that house is spotless by the time we return." She says.

"Of course." I tell her.

I can hear in the background, Roger calling her 'Babe' and for her to come over to wherever he was at.

She then hung up and I pressed the 'End' button and right as I turned around to set down my phone back onto the counter, I see Ashton leaning against the doorway to the kitchen.

"Were those your parents?" He asked.

"Yeah." I reply while trying to hide the fear I was feeling.

"Are you okay?" He asks.

"I'm fine." I tell him with a convincing smile, hopefully.

He starts walking up to me and gently places his hand on the side of my face and out of habit, I flinched a little bit. Then quickly became wide-eyed as I hoped he hadn't noticed. All I kept doing was repeating to myself in my head that I hoped he didn't ask questions.

"My god. I'm not gonna hurt you." He says with sympathy. "If you want, you can stay with me and just tell your parents that you're staying with a friend." He tells me.

"Thanks. But my mom and her boyfriend won't be back from her business trip until next month." I tell him.

"So you'll be here by yourself?" He asks concerned.

"Yeah, but it's okay." I assure him with a smile.

"No it's not. You shouldn't be staying here by yourself. It isn't safe." He tells me.

"I'll be fine. I have pepper spray and a baseball bat." I tell him.

He chuckles. "Baby no. And if you don't want to stay with me at my place, then I'll stay here with you." He says while looking me in my eyes.

"Okay." I smile at him.

"Good." He smiles and gives me another kiss.

My god I can just kiss him forever. I wonder what he'd be like in bed. Oh my god, I need to stop. One step at a time horn dog. I mentally tell myself.

We both soon discover that we are really tired and feel we need to go to bed.

So after turning off the TV, he asks me where the extra blankets are so he could sleep on the couch.

I can't believe the words that were about to come out of my mouth.

"You can sleep in my room if you want. The bed will be more comfortable than the couch." I suggest.

"Are you sure you'd be comfortable with that?" He asks me.

I nod my head and then we start to make our way upstairs and since I'm already in PJ's and he has no clothes here, he ends up asking me first if I'd be okay if he could sleep in his boxers.

I was thinking about it for a moment and didn't realize I was thinking about it too long until I heard him say something.

"Actually, that was stupid of me. Of course I'll sleep in my clothes. Sorry." He says.

"No." I tell him a little quicker than I wanted to reply. "Sorry. You can sleep in your boxers if you want to." I assure him with a smile.

"Okay." He chuckles. "Tomorrow I'll be sure to grab PJ's along with some other clothes." He smiles and winks at me causing me to blush.

We both get underneath the blankets and then he asks me something I never thought I would ever hear from a guy.

"Is it okay if I can hold you as we fall asleep?" He asks.

"I'd like that." I smile at him.

I then lay on my side and feel him interlace his fingers with mine as he takes hold of my hand while bringing his arm around my waist and moving close to me to where I can feel his chest hit my back.

It was like our bodies seemed to mold and fit perfectly together.

I can't believe this has happened but either way, I love it.

CHAPTER 10: The Next Morning

ASHTON

Waking up this morning, I had felt like maybe I had dreamed about what happened. However, when I open my eyes and see that I have the most beautiful woman sleeping in my arms, I know it's real.

I tried hard not to wake her up but before I even had a chance to get up myself or slowly slide my arm out from under her head, I saw her begin to move a little bit and wake up.

She moved her head and looked up at me as I looked down at her and smiled before leaning my head down to kiss her.

"Morning beautiful." I tell her.

"Morning." She smiles.

"Want some breakfast?" I ask.

"Sounds good. What would you like me to make?" She asks.

"Baby, I'm gonna cook us breakfast. So don't worry. You just wake up some more and breakfast will be done soon." I tell her.

"Okay." She blushes.

"You look so cute when you blush and I'm glad I do that to you." I smile at her.

She bites her lip a little and then I give her one more kiss before getting up and heading down to the kitchen to start making breakfast.

Once breakfast was over, Daisy and I went over to my apartment to grab some of my stuff to take back to her place and then after coming back, we mostly hung out at the house the rest of the day and night and during dinner, I felt like she was a little bit worried about something.

"Is everything okay?" I ask her.

"Yeah. It's just, how are we going to keep this from everyone? We wont be able to go anywhere or do anything together." She says.

I look at her and think about how right she is because everyone is everywhere. Everyone goes to the same mall, movie theaters and restaurants.

I interlace our hands together and have her look at me.

"Baby, I would never want to put you through anything you didn't want to do and I am not embarrassed or ashamed of us. But if it'll make you more comfortable, since the school, other than the principal and them don't know where I live, we can always stay at my place. Also, I was thinking, if you want to, since there's a four day weekend coming up, maybe you'd want to go away with me to a cabin that I like to go to when I want to get away." I suggest. "I know it might be soon, but I figured since the holiday weekend is coming up in a few weeks, then maybe you'd want to go and we can be alone without any distractions."

"Can I think about it? I mean, I do want to be with you but, to go to a cabin with you when we just started seeing each other, I just..." I stop her.

"I know, it sounds creepy. But I swear, that no matter if we go to the cabin or stay here, I want to spend every moment I can with you." I assure her with a smile.

"Okay." She replies with a smile.

We lean in and give each other a kiss on the lips before doing the dishes and heading off to bed.

****

The weekend went by faster than the both of us wanted it to and today was gonna be the first time we went to school and had to try our best not to be too obvious about the fact we're dating.

Here's the thing, there's nothing more that I would like to do than to show everyone I am dating Daisy. But she said she was worried about me losing my job and I told her I didn't care but then she told me she wanted to not risk it. So because she's saying not to say anything, I'm not. Although we both agreed that she could tell her best friend, Janet.

Her birthday is next month and already I am thinking about what to get her.

Sure this might all sound too soon but when I really like a girl, I go all in. May be too soon but I don't care, she's worth it.

It was really hard getting through class I'll admit, seeing as to how I couldn't stop looking at her and making her blush whenever she caught me looking at her.

For last period, as soon as she came walking inside the classroom, I made sure she closed the door and locked it as we we went towards the back to where we couldn't be seen to where I pushed her gently up against the cabinet doors in the back and we began making out.

For the next couple of weeks it was getting harder and harder for the both of us to keep from touching one another in class.

I can't wait for the cabins, if she decides to go with me. This way, we can both be alone and can go outside in public, even to the store and not worry about people staring and looking at us and reporting it to the authorities that she's my student. Luckily she also looks mature for her age as well as acts like that too.

My god, what is she doing to me?

CHAPTER 11: The Cabin

DAISY

So I have decided to go to the cabin with Ashton.

For the last few weeks, we have seemed to have gotten more affectionate with one another and we both seem to feel the same way about each other.

I'm not sure in how this will all work out in the end but all I know is that for now, I'm going to enjoy every minute of this while I can.

After grabbing some groceries for the cabin and snacks for the road, since it would take only a couple of hours to get there, we started heading up and I started thinking about how I feel like one of those girls in the movies where their boyfriend asks them to go away with them to the countryside or something like that and they have a romantic weekend without a care in the world. I hope that's what it's like. So far so good.

Once we arrived and started to head inside the cabin, I couldn't help but think of how beautiful everything looked.

It definiteley was private and there wasn't many things or even other people around for at least a few miles.

I was glad that we had already unpacked and had gone grocery shopping because I didn't want to have to go anywhere but the lake or around here.

For our first night here, he decided to order some pizza and have us cuddle up afterwards by the fire while in each other's arms underneath the blanket.

Everything was perfect and really romantic. I was so glad that I had found someone like him that I felt safe with and that I felt I had a connection with.

I felt him gently caress my arm a little bit and I'm not sure why but it sent chills up and down my spine in a good way.

Then as he does that, I get so caught up in the moment that I start to rub his thigh a little bit while we both continue to look at the fire.

I then feel him place gentle kisses on the side of my neck, causing me to tilt my head more to the side so he has more access. His hands and lips feel amazing.

Am I ready for this? Am I ready to have sex with him? My god he feels so good. I can tell he has done this before and if he's making me feel this way now without doing anything, I can only imagine what he'd be like inside of me. Just the thought of that makes me wet and start to moan a little bit.

I tilt my head back a little bit and wrap my arm around the back of his head to lean his head closer as I turn to look at him and we start kissing each other deeply.

I then feel his hand move up inside my shirt, lifting it up a little bit while moving his hand into my bra and starts caressing one of my soft breasts and then gently squeezing the tip of my nipple which causes me to bite my lower lip from the instant pleasure I get.

I start to move my hand further up his thigh until I feel the outside of his bulge and as I begin rubbing it, I hear him start to moan as I next feel his hand move into my pants and then sliding his fingers into my panties as he begins slowly and gently at first, rubbing my clit while sliding his fingers in and out between my wet folds.

Then I stop his hand real quick and try to catch my breath.

"Wait." I tell him.

"I'm sorry baby." He says. "I swear I would never force you to do anything you don't want to do." He says to me.

"It's just, do you have a condom?" I ask.

"Of course." He smiles.

"Okay then." I reply and pull his head closer to me again and we start kissing each other and removing each other's clothes one piece at a time until we both are naked and he's laying on top of me underneath the blankets and I watch as he finishes rolling on the condom and then gently interlaces our fingers and raising my hands and his above my head before he slowly starts to enter the tip of his fully erect cock in side of me a little at a time until his full length is inside of me and at first I gasp and yelp a little from the pain as he begins sliding in and out of me slowly until the pain dissipates and I feel nothing but pleasure.

Once I begin to moan a little more I start to ask him to go faster. And we both moan and he grunts as he gets closer to his climax which is close to the same time as mine.

Then with his final thrusts and grunts, we both release at the same time with our bodies from the heat of the fire and of course our bodies getting hot from our movements.

We catch our breaths and lay down still on the blankets in each other's arms until we finally fall asleep telling each other 'I love you.'

CHAPTER 12: I'm Falling Hard

ASHTON

We had so much fun here at the cabins and the day after tomorrow, both her and I were leaving back to her place.

Tonight I made it a special night by making us some dinner where we ate at the dining table with no other lighting than the candles I lit to create a more intimate and romantic dinner.

We were talking and getting to know one another more.

Everything was going great and she was telling me what she wanted to do after school. Things were fine up until I soon realized that I touched on a sensitive topic.

"So your parents must be proud." I smiled.

The smile on her face and the energy in the room seemed to have both disappeared at the same time.

"I haven't told them." She says under her breath.

"Why not?" I asked.

"Because they don't care and they would try everything in their power to keep that from happening." She says while finishing her soda.

I could tell by the look on her face that she didn't want to talk about them although I was very curious to hear about them but I didn't want to upset her or make her feel uncomfortable in any way, so I dropped it.

"What about your parents? I bet they're proud their son went to college and became a teacher." She smiles while trying to change the subject.

"Not exactly." I chuckle as I drink the last of my wine.

"What do you mean?" She asks.

"Well my parents always wanted me to take over my dad's company and after I graduated high school I told him I wanted to be a teacher. Of course that pissed him off but then eventually he came around. Although my mom was all for me becoming a teacher since the beginning." I smile at her.

"Well that's good." She smiles.

"Yeah." I reply with a smile while looking at her.

She catches me staring at her and starts blushing.

So I get up and walk over slowly towards her, lean down and place my hands on each side of the arm of her chair and press my lips onto hers.

The kiss starts off slow and passionate at first. Then quickly gets more heated as she wraps both her arms around my neck and while still kissing, I wrap my arms around her waist as she begins to stand.

We pull our lips apart for a moment to catch our breaths.

"I'm sorry. I just find it hard to control myself around you." I tell her.

"Me too." She tells me.

I gently caress the side of her face with my hand while looking into her eyes.

She then pulls me in closer to kiss me and again the kiss gets heated up quickly as I start moving my hands down her lower back and as soon as I go lower and grab her ass she moans even more into my mouth and we end up making love to each other before falling asleep in each other's arms.

When we woke up the next morning, I was not looking forward to it because I knew that the day after tomorrow we had to go back to school and be more careful around each other.

I ended up staying with him and we both became more affectionate and playful with each other. In fact, I didn't feel like I was dating my teacher but more like I was with someone a few years older than me who I had met somewhere one day.

I feel like both him and I are unstoppable together. Like nothing could ruin this moment.

I never thought I would ever find someone who would want me the way he does. He's not embarrassed or even ashamed to be with me. He helps me see my worth and give me confidence. I'm on top of the world with an amazing man that I feel I'm falling for.

CHAPTER 13: Making Texts Reality

DAISY

One week had gone by when we had returned from the cabins and also had returned to school.

Things were different as this was after we slept together and had all that freedom around at the cabin for us to touch one another and not have to worry about people finding out. Now, we needed to be more careful.

He kept sending me texts throughout class everyday though.

ASHTON: I want to kiss you so badly right now!

ME: I know. I want that too! ;)

ASHTON: I want to see you after class....there's something I would like to discuss with you. ;)

ME: Anything for you Mr. Moon

ASHTON: Okay, I'm liking the way you say my name like that. I can only imagine you calling me that while I'm bending you over.

ME: Have I been a bad girl?

ASHTON: Very bad!

The bell rang before we could finish our steamy and sexy texting session.

Damn he has made me wet with just thinking about his hands all over me as memories of those few times we were intimate together, started flashing through my head.

After school, I did as I was told, I went straight to his classroom and right as soon as I walked in about to say something sexual, I stopped when I saw the principal talking with Ashton.

"Daisy." The Principal said while turning and looking at me.

"Mr. Weathers." I replied while the pit of my stomach began feeling queasy as I felt nervous as hell.

"What are you doing here?" Mr. Weathers asked me.

"I come here after school everyday because I am trying to raise my grade and Mr. Moon said that if I help him he would raise it." I tell him. Which wasn't a lie.

"Oh. Alright then. I will leave you guys to it." He says while starting to head out the classroom when he stops in the doorway and looks back at Ashton. "Remember what I told you."

"Yes. I'll have an answer for you soon." Ashton says reassuring.

Mr. Weathers doesn't say anything just winks at me and then leaves while closing the door behind him. Which was good as I could finally let out the breath I had been holding in.

"What was that about?" I asked hesitantly, thinking it was about us and that somehow Mr. Weathers had found out about us.

"Nothing." He smiles at me. "Now, come here." He says while tapping his hand on his lap.

I begin to blush a little bit while I start walking over towards him and he pulls me down onto his lap, making me wrap both my arms around his shoulders as he begins kissing my neck at first and then begins kissing his way up to my lips where we begin making out for what seems like forever. (I mean that in a good way, of course).

Then right as he begins rubbing my thighs a little bit, we both begin to moan in each others' mouths and as his hand begins moving towards my inner thighs, I stop him for a second.

"Wait. We need to lock the door." I tell him.

"That won't matter after they hear you anyways." He says against my lips.

"I'm serious." I giggle.

"Alright baby." He kisses me again and then has me stand up while he goes to lock both the front door and the door in the back.

Then when he turns back around to face me, he looks at me with lust and hunger in his eyes while licking his lips a little bit as he begins walking up to me.

Once he comes closer towards me, he starts rubbing between my thighs over my jeans and I hear him growl low.

"I hate these. Take them off. I can't punish you the right way until you take them off." He says.

"Yes, Sir." I reply.

I then stand up and start unbuttoning my jeans and start pulling them down to my ankles and stepping out of them before tossing them off to the side somewhere and he kisses me slowly on the lips and moans again in my mouth. Then I feel him grip onto one of my arms and quickly turns me around to where I'm facing the window and he has me lay my upper part of my body over his desk while having me hold onto each side of the desk top as he roughly pulls my panties off of me and then pulls my hips and ass out more bent over closer to him.

"You've been a very bad girl today." He begins to tell me as he rubs one of my ass cheeks. "The way you were teasing me earlier in the class with you licking your lips and the way you looked at me while teasing me with that pen in your mouth." He says to me.

"I'm sorry Sir." I tell him.

"Mmmm. It's too late Princess." He says as I feel him lift his hand off before smacking my ass cheek hard but not enough to leave a mark.

"Ah." I yelp while quickly covering my mouth with one of my hands to make sure that nobody hears me.

"Shh." He says as he leans closer down to my ear and gently places his hand over the front of my neck to make me look back at him with my ass still against his hard member that's more than ready to break free from his pants.

We start kissing one another and then he smacks my butt a couple of more times before he gently moves his hand from my neck and moves it down to my wet sex and begins rubbing my clit slowly at first while continuing to place kisses on my back until I can't take it anymore and stand up and quickly turn to face him and start making out with him before I start undoing his pants and pulling them down along with his boxers and then having him sit down on his chair while I get down in front of him on both my knees and start slowly stroking his cock with my hand as I slowly start putting his tip inside my mouth at first until I take in more of his hard throbbing cock until I feel the tip hit the back of my throat. Which as soon as I heard him moan from that, I then begin bobbing my head up and down a little more, enjoying every inch of him in my mouth as he grabs my hair and moans.

Then he lifts my head up and has me stand before taking my shirt off and bra then tossing them off to the side and laying me on my back on top of his desk while he bends down and takes out a condom from his pocket and goes back to kissing me after tearing it open with his teeth and rolling it on his full length.

He starts kissing down my neck while cupping my breasts in his hands and taking one of my nipples in his mouth one at at time until he makes his way down to my wet sex and gets down on his knees and leans in to begin licking my clit and pleasuring me beyond ecstasy as he moves his tongue up and down my sensitive area and surprising me by thrusting a finger inside of me and moving in and out faster and faster until I come undone in front of him while covering my mouth to keep my moans from being heard by anyone.

When he's finished licking up my juices, he kisses his way back up to my lips to have me taste myself on his mouth before thrusting inside of me so hard that I accidentally let out a loud yelp of pleasure but thankfully he was quick to notice that he smashes his lips back onto mine while thrusting faster and harder into me. Wrapping both my legs around his waist to allow him to go in even deeper to where I can feel the tip of him hit my G Spot with every thrust.

Between the both of us moaning, panting and gripping onto one another as he claims me as his, I come and after one final thrust, he comes as well, filling up the condom with his seed before collapsing on top of me, out of breath and with both my legs and arms still wrapped around him.

CHAPTER 14: The Best Date

ASHTON

Daisy is so amazing and unique. I can't believe at how mature she is for her age. She is beautiful inside and out and she makes me so happy.

After our amazing moment we had in the classroom a couple weeks ago, we both decided that we may not be so lucky next time. Especially with how loud she is. So we decided to skip the after school thing and go right back to her place.

Today however, she was acting a little different than normal. Almost like she was bothered by something. Oh my god, I hope she isn't pregnant. Not because I wouldn't want kids with her but I just don't want her to be bullied even more over that.

So after dinner while we were sitting on the couch watching TV and cuddling, I decided to ask her.

"What's wrong baby?" I ask.

"Nothing." She replies sadly.

"Come on. You can tell me." I assure her with a kiss on the head.

She then sits up and looks down at her lap as she takes in a deep breath and then let it out before she starts.

"It's just that, my mom and her boyfriend are coming back home next Tuesday and I'm not sure..." She begins but I stop her as I see she's on the verge of tears.

"Hey. It's okay. If you want, I can talk with them." I suggest.

"No. You don't understand. They aren't like most parents. They will find a way to destroy your life just as they have mine." She tells me.

"What do you mean, like yours?" I asked worriedly.

"My mother is not the nurturing kind and her boyfriend is just as bad. They are cruel people that get pleasure out of hurting others. Including me. So if they heard about you and me, your job and your reputation will be down the drain. Not to mention they would try and press charges against you, just to get back at me." She tells me.

"Hmmm. Well then, since you're gonna be eighteen tomorrow anyways, you can do whatever you want. To which then you can come and live with me. We can move your things out this weekend and there's nothing they can do about it. Also, even if they did find out about us, they wouldn't have much to go on if we told them you were eighteen when we started dating and they wouldn't even have to know about us having sex together. So the worst that could really happen is that yes, I could lose my job, but I don't care, I can still teach at other places." I try to assure her. Which wasn't entirely a lie.

She looks at me with a surprised look on her face.

"Are you asking me to move in with you?" She asks.

"Yes. I am." I smile.

She doesn't say anything and at first I begin thinking that she might be getting ready to say no but then I see a smile forming on her face, the biggest I have ever seen on hers and she throws her arms around me, causing me to fall back on the couch with her on top of me, kissing me all over my face and lips in excitement.

"I would love to." She says with a lot of excitement in her voice.

"Good. Then we should get packing tomorrow." I chuckled.

"The hell with that. Let's start tonight." She laughs.

Though right as she gets up and grabs my hand to have us go towards the bedroom to start packing, we don't even get through folding a few of her clothes before putting them in one of her suitcases when we both end up moving all the bags off the bed and onto the floor before making love. What can I say, she's hard to resist.

****

When the next day arrived, it was her birthday and luckily fell on a Saturday which meant no school.

So I had planned a whole day of doing whatever she wanted to do (go to the movies, out to lunch, etc) yet all she wanted to do was make sure she was moved out of her house.

She didn't have a lot to pack so it didn't take us all day long to pack and unload her things into my apartment. Which meant we still had some daylight out and I really wanted her to have fun in doing something she wanted to do to celebrate.

When she decided what she wanted to do, I was real excited and yet surprised at the same time. She wanted to grab something to eat and then go to the local drive-in left that's one of few left in the world and go see two movies.

I was real excited cause I haven't been to one before and had always seen them in the movies I would watch with my grandmother when I was younger and always thought it'd be cool.

So we grabbed a couple of blankets, ordered a couple of sandwiches from a nice deli in town, grabbed some drinks and snacks then headed down.

We had parked in the back and instead of having those old fashioned speakers that you hang on your window, they had it to where you can listen to the movie through your car speakers by tuning into a certain station.

So as we did that and waited for the movie to start, we cuddled up next to one another and fed each other a few bites of things and then snuggled up under the blanket together when the movie started.

The first movie was pretty action packed and the second one was scary a little bit but we didn't get to finish it, she had fallen asleep during the middle of the second movie. So we headed home and laid in our new bed (formerly known as: my bed), and before falling asleep in each other's arms, I kissed her goodnight and wished her one final time, a Happy Birthday. To which she replied with a 'thank you' and fell asleep.

I felt almost like a teenage boy from the fifties by taking her to the drive-in but I have gotta say that this was the best date I had ever been on in my life, hands down.

CHAPTER 15: So Much For Happiness

DAISY

Things have been going great and I loved it how Ashton always picked me up from work every night and greeted me with a kiss. Although for some reason, I still felt a little nervous about my mom and her boyfriend coming back today and thinking about their reaction after seeing I wasn't there anymore.

I mean, sure I was eighteen and legally could move out without them having a say in it as well as the fact that I at least left them a note.

Besides, I'm sure if anything, they'll be overjoyed that I'm not living there anymore. I'll be out of their hair and they can go on about their lives just as they always have only with an extra spare room.

Graduation was only a couple of months away and I was really excited as was Ashton also. Mostly cause he told me this morning while making me breakfast, that he was thinking that whether or not I decided to go to college, he was planning on taking a job offer he received a couple of weeks ago and was thinking about taking but wasn't sure because he wanted to make sure I would go with him. Which of course I told him I would love to. So of course we celebrated and hugged as well as kissed one another.

However, just when my life started to seem like it was coming together, I had suddenly felt nauseous and had to excuse myself from my third period class.

Ugh....Please tell me I'm not getting the flu. Hopefully it's just food poisoning or something like that. I can't handle being sick right now.

I didn't eat lunch cause almost everything I looked at caused me to be sick and almost made me puke so I just grabbed a granola bar there and some water and headed towards Ashton's classroom to see if he had anything that could settle my stomach.

However, when I got up to his door, I heard a woman giggling and Ashton talking lowly to some woman. I didn't want to jump to conclusions so I opened the door to make sure it wasn't what I thought it was but sure enough, it was EXACTLY what I thought it was.

I saw him and some thin woman with fake big tits and dark hair, with her hands around his neck, kissing him and him not pushing her away.

I tried not to cry or make a sound but my hands had other plans as both the now half-eaten-granola and water bottle dropped to the ground as I just froze in place, while staring at something that instantly broke my heart as I could feel the pain.

They both look up at me and I right away begin crying uncontrollably and start immediately running out from the school while ignoring Ashton calling out for me.

Once I was off school grounds, I stopped at a park nearby there and I started catching my breath while trying to think about what I just saw and what I should do next.

Suddenly I began to feel sick again and bent over and threw up. Then as I wiped my mouth after I was done, I sat down with my back against the tree for a few hours, not realizing how long I've been sitting here and tried pulling myself together and figuring out what I was going to do next until I finally came to the conclusion that I had better grab my things from his apartment and hoped he would not be home yet seeing as to how, school wasn't going to be out for another hour.

So I call a cab to take me to his apartment so I could grab my things and while on my way over there, I called up Janet to see if I could at least stay the night for just tonight.

When she picked up, I just came right out and asked her if I could stay the night with her and explained everything to her in a shorter version. She told me I could stay with her for as long as I wanted to and not to worry about anything. So I thanked her and then right as the cab arrived in front of the apartment duplex, I got out and asked the driver to stay there while I grabbed my things.

Although right as I took the elevator up to the fourth floor and got out to walk towards his apartment, I saw my bags not just already packed but also, out in the hallway as though they were tossed out. I suddenly became filled with rage and was not going to leave without demanding an explanation. I at least deserved that much.

I knocked on the door a few times until finally, after a minute, the door opened up and standing right there looking at me with disgust, was the bimbo who I saw making out with Ashton.

"Can I help you?" She asked me in a bitchy tone.

"I need to speak with Ashton." I tell her although it's none of her business really.

"I'm sorry little girl but he wants nothing to do with you and if you ever come near my fiance again, I will make sure that you get charged with stalking him and I." She smirks.

'Fiance'? Is that what she just told me?

It was like I got punched in the stomach yet again and I wanted to cry but forced the tears back into my eyes as I did not want to give this bitch the satisfaction. So I just quickly removed my key to the place and handed it to her.

"Here! Can you at least give him this?" I asked her assertively.

"Thanks." She says as she rips it out of my hand. "Now, grab your shit and leave us the hell alone!" She says before slamming the door in my face.

I frustratingly grabbed my few bags that I had, along with my messenger bag that had my school things in it and went back downstairs to the cab where I asked the driver to then take me to Janet's place.

Wow, just when I thought school life couldn't get any worse. (Note the sarcasm).

CHAPTER 16: You Don't Know Who I Am

ASHTON

It's been almost two weeks since I was surprised by my ex girlfriend who somehow found me who cheated on me a couple years ago on the same night I was going to propose to her.

She took my heart and she ripped it out of me and it became the worst pain I had ever felt, or at least thought I would ever feel until I saw the look on Daisy's face when Melrose had forced herself on me and kissed me right as the door opened up and I saw Daisy.

I pushed Melrose off of me but by the time I tried to run after Daisy, she was already gone and so I kicked Melrose out of the classroom and waited til school was over before I had gone looking for Daisy but had no such luck. I ended up looking for her until nine at night but I couldn't find her.

So with hopes that she might be back at the apartment and would hopefully be waiting there for me so that I could explain that it really wasn't what it looked like, but when I got there, I as greeted instead with Melrose and all of Daisy's things were gone.

"What the fuck are you doing here Melrose? How the hell did you find me even?" I asked her.

"Well, I missed you baby. Then once I heard from your parents where you were at, I just had to come and see you." She says pretending to sound all innocent.

"Well you need to leave. We aren't together anymore and we will never be together again. So I'm gonna only say this once. Get the hell out of my life and stay out before I put a restraining order on you just as I did with my parents." I tell her.

"Seriously?!" She snaps. "Is this about that fat student of yours that has a crush on you?" She asks with folded arms and while glaring at me.

"What? Okay, first of all, she's curvy, NOT fat. And second of all, yes. I'm in love with her and I've been out looking for her this entire time." I tell her.

"Oh, well, she came by earlier all upset. She told me to let you know that she never wanted to see you again and that if you ever came near her again that she would have a restraining order put on you. So she came in to grab her things and then left." She says again with that annoyingly fake innocent demeanor.

"I don't believe you. So get the fuck out! I mean it!" I snap at her as I stomped back towards the door and opened it up for her to leave.

"You can't kick me out. You and I belong together." She says.

"Bullshit. You never gave two shits about me Melrose. You are a harlot that wanted to be with me just for the money because my parents were loaded. You even gave me shit for wanting to be a teacher cause you were afraid I wouldn't have enough money for us. Hell, you didn't even want kids." I reminded her.

"And you think that sleeping with one is better?" She fires at me although from the immediate look on her face right now, I could tell she was surprised herself she said anything.

"I. Said. Get. Out." I tell her again through gritted teeth.

She huffs and she puffs and grabs her purse as she storms out of the apartment while yelling back to me down the hallway that I will regret this decision.

My god she is so pathetic. However, I have to now focus on trying to find Daisy and try to explain to her in what really happened.

For the next few days, she has been absent from class, wasn't returning any of my texts or calls and worst of all, had even taken some sick days off of work. Although Janet always ignored me every time I had gone into where she worked at and was always told that Daisy wasn't there. In fact, if it wasn't for the manager the other day telling me she was off work for a while cause she was sick, I never would have known anything.

I understand why she'd be upset and how easily she could have thought what she did when she saw Melrose and I that day but, still, I didn't want her to think that Melrose meant anything to me and that we were back together cause we weren't.

Finally, when Friday had arrived, I saw her coming into class a little late and placed down a note for being late and sat down at a desk that wasn't in the middle, closer towards me but in the back corner where I could barely see her.

I was of course happy to see her but also upset a little bit when I wasn't able to look at her beautiful face. This was all my fault and I had needed to find a way to at least explain to her the truth. Rather she believed me or not or even was willing to give me another chance, it didn't matter. She deserved to at least know the truth.

So I waited until the bell rang and as all the kids began walking out, I noticed she was one of the last ones.

"Daisy?" I called out.

She stopped and it took a moment before she turned around to look at me.

"Yes, Mr. Moon?" She answers while avoiding eye contact.

"How are you?" I asked even though right after I said it I realized what a stupid question it was.

"I'm fine." She says.

"Look, I wanted to talk with you about..." I began but she stopped me.

"Please. I'd rather not hear about it. I really don't care what you tell me cause either way, it'll most likely be bullshit and I really have enough going on that the last thing I need is to hear about you and some bimbo. So if you'll excuse me, I need to get to my next class." She says right before she turns around and heads out.

CHAPTER 17: Plans Changed

A Month Later.....

DAISY

I didn't care what he had to say. It would be the same as all the other people that lie about why they cheated on the one's they supposedly 'loved' or 'liked a lot'. It's always the same old shit and I'm sick of it. Plus, I'm really not in the mood and really do have a lot on my plate at the moment seeing as to how I recently found out I was pregnant. Yeah, perfect timing, right?

After school was over, Janet was nice enough to give me a ride to work. She has been nice enough to keep her offer as it stood the first night I stayed with her as in I could stay with her for however long I wanted to since her parents are rarely ever home anyways and the fact that they wouldn't care.

So I finally took her up on that offer and took her spare bedroom and we were now roommates. She is so awesome and is like the sister I never had.

Tonight, since Summer was coming, I needed to try and stock a few things to prepare for the big Summer blow out sale we always have with towels, decor and other Summer themed things for the household and yards.

In fact, I was in an aisle, trying to put back some bins onto the third shelf when one of the bins almost fell back onto me as I quickly realized I hadn't pushed it far enough onto the shelf to have it stay.

Before the bin could hit me, I saw someone's arms catch it and then pushed back up onto the shelf for me.

When I looked to see who it was and thank them, I immediately turned around to start walking towards the back in the opposite direction after I saw it was Ashton.

"Hey." He says as he stops me by grabbing my hand and has me turn to face him.

"No." I tell him as I yank my arms out from his grasp.

"Please, give me a chance to explain." He started.

"No. In case you didn't understand what I told you a month ago, I'll repeat it one last time. I don't give a fuck about you and some bitch. Therefore I don't want to hear about what 'happened.' Actions speak louder than words and your actions by god, they spoke really loud.

Please leave before I have security escort you out." I tell him while trying not to cry. Fucking hormones.

I quickly head off towards the back and hide in there for a while until I see that he's gone. That's when I let all the pain and tears come out.

"I'm so sorry little man or girl." I start talking to my belly. "Mommy didn't mean to curse at your daddy. I'm sorry I messed up in that department. But I promise you that I'll take good care of you along with your aunt Janet."

I then head back to work after collecting myself and go on the rest of the night without thinking about what just happened.

~~~~~~~~~~~~~~~~~~~

The next day at school, I had come in for second period and was eating some crackers to settle my stomach.

Then when lunchtime came around, I was walking towards the cafeteria when all of a sudden, I felt somebody trip me.

I tried landing on my hands to prevent me from landing on my stomach but it was too late. Right away, I held onto my stomach as I rolled over to see who tripped me.

"Awww, did the fat girl hurt her disgusting belly?" Vicki spat out.

"Fuck off!" I tell her as I am now pissed that she may have caused me to have a miscarriage and right before she can do anything else, I hear Janet come up from behind her.
~~~~~~~~~~~~~~~~~~~

"She told you to fuck off bitch!" Janet says as she pushes Vicki out of the way and drops to her knees to try and help me up.

"Are you okay?" She asks.

"I think so. But I think I might need to go to the hospital." I tell her as I hold my stomach in pain.

She starts to help me up and she glares at Vicki while we walk past her and her POSSE.

"It's gonna be okay, we're gonna get you to the hospital. Everything will be alright." She tries to assure me when we both know there's a chance I might have miscarried since it has only been a few weeks that I've been pregnant.

I was worried all throughout the ride to the hospital that as soon as we walked inside, Janet demanded one of the nurses to come and help me and was screaming at them as they practically were doing their job in asking some standardized questions. But Janet didn't care, she wanted me to be checked out immediately.

Which I was and thankfully, after being thoroughly checked, I was told the baby was fine and wasn't harmed.

I felt a huge sense of relief knowing that that whore didn't hurt or kill my baby.

The doctor had sent me home after having me stay there for a few more hours just to make sure everything was one hundred percent good before sending me back home.

Then once we got back to the place I just laid in my bed, rubbed my belly, thanking god for not letting my baby get hurt or die and then cried myself to sleep.

While on the way home, both Janet and I felt it might be better if I had stayed home for the next couple of weeks and she would let the teachers all know that I was sick and that I needed to just have my assignments sent to me through EMAIL.

I felt like I needed to be in a bubble until the baby arrived. I could do home school and finish my year that way. I never cared anyways about Prom and the whole graduation thing. Okay maybe not the graduation part. I have always wanted to hear my name being called up as I walked up on the stage and I shook the principal's hand, grabbed my diploma and be able to say that I did it. However, it looks as though plans might have changed.

CHAPTER 18: Fingers Crossed

ASHTON

As I'm sitting in my classroom during lunchtime, I can't stop thinking about Daisy and how much I love her. I can't even eat or sleep, it's that bad.

While trying to grade a few papers to catch up, I suddenly hear a couple of girls yelling at each other that sounded like they were fighting.

So as I got up and opened my door to see what was going on, I saw Janet and Daisy walking towards the opposite end with Daisy holding her stomach in pain.

What the hell happened I thought to myself. That is until I looked and noticed Vicki and her idiotic friends were laughing as Janet and Daisy were leaving.

I stomped up towards Vicki and turned her around to face me.

"Mr. Moon?" She gasped.

"Come with me. You're going to explain to Mr. Weathers, what you just did to Daisy." I tell her as I take hold of her arm and we begin walking down the hallway towards the office.

"Mr. Moon, I can explain." She begins before I cut her off.

"Save it for the Principal and hopefully Daisy won't press assault charges against you." I tell her with a smirk even though I didn't see exactly what had happened however, I know how she treats Daisy and that bullying bullshit stops right here and now.

So after she got done spilling out her guts in how she has been treating Daisy, including with what she did today, in which I wanted to punch something so hard right now after hearing her doing that.

Now, of course, I had to threaten Vicki's grade in order for her to confess everything, but still, it was great seeing justice being served and a bully being punished for their crimes.

When school ended, I wanted to check in on Daisy. Even if she didn't want to talk to me, I still wanted to make sure that she was alright. And not to sound like a stalker or anything, I looked up the address to Janet's house before heading on over with a bouquet of flowers.

Once I arrived and knocked on the door, Janet answered and had a look of anger on her face.

"What the hell do you want Mr. Moon?" She demanded.

"I wanted to check on Daisy. I heard she got hurt." I begin to say.

"Yes, she did. She's fine now, thanks for asking. I'll let her know you stopped by." She says and slams the door in front of my face, Not giving me a chance to say anything.

I'm not giving up though. I'm gonna continue to try and talk with Daisy because I'm in love with her and I know that she's in love with me still.

I had received an EMAIL later on tonight from Daisy that was sent to all her teachers in seeing how she had not felt too good and was going to need her work to be sent to her through EMAIL for the next two weeks.

I wondered what was going on? Was she alright? How bad was that kick? Damnit, I don't hit girls but I swear, I would make an exception for Vicki.

For the next couple of days, I have glanced every so often over towards Daisy's seat and just sigh as I noticed each time that she wasn't there.

Then today, I saw Janet and finally had the guts to grab her attention to ask her about Daisy. At least just to let me know she's okay.

"Janet?" I called out to her in the hallway during lunch while she was talking with a few friends.

She looked at me for a minute and then said goodbye to her friends before walking up towards me in my classroom.

"Yes, Mr. Moon?" She asks irritated.

"I know that Daisy wants nothing to do with me or to even let me explain about that day that she saw me with another woman. But I swear on my life that I would never do anything to purposely hurt her. Melrose showed up out of nowhere and as soon as she kissed me, that's when Daisy saw us kissing but didn't even stay long enough to watch me push Melrose away. But anyways, I do love her and I know she hates me but, can you at least tell me she's okay?" I asked with pleading eyes.

She scowls at me for a moment and then looks away and shakes her head before looking back at me and taking notice the lack of sleep I've had and the couple days of stubble.

"She's okay. I mean, she still loves you. She's just hurt. You really hurt her. And she's gonna kill me for even telling you this but..." She stops for a moment to take in a deep breath and let it out before continuing. "She's pregnant. And that day when Vicki kicked her hard in the stomach, we went to the hospital to make sure the baby was okay and it is. She's okay too. She just needs a couple of weeks off." She finishes.

"Thanks. Wait, what?" I ask her while in shock. Did she just say that Daisy was pregnant? I'm gonna be a dad?

"Yeah well, I'm gonna go and grab a bite to eat before my next period. See ya." Janet says.

"Oh, wait!" I called out to her. "Do you think I can see her? Just for a couple of minutes?" I ask her.

She glares at me and thinks about it for a moment it looks like, before she answers me.

"Fine. I'm going to work right after school. You can stop by the house then. But I promise you that if you do or say anything to upset her, I will personally kill you and make sure that nobody can find your body, you get me?" She threatens.

Now even though she's younger than me, I still am freaked out a little bit as she sounds serious and looks as though she can 'take care of business' if needed.

"I promise." I reply before thanking her.

"Yeah, yeah. Just don't make me regret this." She says while walking towards the door and then stops to look back at me for a minute, "Oh and please don't let her know I told you about all of this. Including the part where I tell you about the spare house key that's underneath the plant in the pot that's to the left of the door." She smirks and then continues to leave.

Okay, this was gonna be it. After school, I was going to make sure that I made everything better or at least tried to. Fingers crossed.

CHAPTER 19: This Should Be Fun.....

DAISY

I have been more tired lately and already my feet are sarting to feel achy and starting to swell a little bit as I'm finding myself having to wear slippers and bigger shoes because they're the only things that fit at the moment. Not to mention my cravings have been a little weird.

I was sitting on the couch, eating some fruit while watching Nine Months and as soon as I begin playing it, I immediately have to pause it as I hear a knock on the door.

Which I know it can't be Janet because she's at work. So I get up and walk to the door but I first ask to see who it is before I open it up.

"It's me, Ashton." He says with a sad tone in his voice.

"What do you want?" I ask.

"Can I please come in and talk to you?" He asks me.

I continue to stand there for a moment debating if whether or not I should let him in and finally, I decide to open up the door.

As soon as I open up the door and look at him standing there, he looks like he hasn't eaten or even slept for a few days. 'Good' I thought. Well, at least some of me is thinking that.

"Come in." I tell him while walking towards the couch and taking a seat.

He shuts the door behind him and walks over towards the couch and sits on the opposite end of the couch from me while I pause the movie.

I can feel him looking at me and seems to be just as nervous as I am.

"How are you?" He asks.

"I'm okay." I tell him.

"I heard you were sick." He says.

"Yeah." I nod my head in agreement. "Well, I thought I was. But I know Janet told you I wasn't sick." I say.

"Well, I'm glad that she did." He says to me.

"Yes, Well, I'm not." I turn and look at him. "How could you do what you did and let that bitch kiss you?" I blurt out.

"I know that it seemed like I was kissing her back but I wasn't. The moment you opened the door was the same time she smashed her lips onto mine and I immediately pushed her away and was going to yell at her but then I saw you. I cared more about trying to explain things to you but you were already gone. Then when I got back home that night, I was hoping to see you when instead, I saw her. Which I'm not sure in how she even got in but after she tried telling me you wanted nothing to do with me anymore and that if I tried to contact you, you would press charges against me..." I stopped him right there.

"Wait, hold up! She said that I would press charges against you? She told me to stay away from you cause you were her fiance." I tell him.

"Yeah well, obviously she's a liar." He nervously chuckles.

"So then who is she and why the hell was she there?" I ask him while deep down I'm worried of what he might tell me. I especially get nervous when I hear him take in a breath and let it out before starting.

"Her and I used to be together. In fact, we were going to get married. But then on the night that I was planning to propose to her, I caught her in bed with who I thought was my best friend at the time. I had later found out that she never really loved me and was only with me because she wanted to get my family's money. Soon after all of that, I found out that both my parents wanted me to take over the family business instead of teaching and thought Melrose could distract me from going to college and she almost did until that night. From then on, I took the money I had in my account, put a restraining order against my parents, for other reasons that weren't just cause of

Melrose, then I left. I even changed my name thinking there was no way they could ever find me. But somehow, I guess my parents found me and then told her where I was and that's how she was able to find me and showed up out of nowhere." He says before turning to look at me and takes both my hands into his and finishes. "But I promise you that I kicked her out and threatened for her to stay out of my life. I love you. I always have and I know that I always will. So please, please, give me another chance to prove it to you." He pleads.

I'm surprised. I never expected him to show up here, let alone talk to me. I had a whole argument that I had been preparing for involving me yelling at him and giving him a piece of my mind. But then he said all of that just now to me. I'm speechless. What should I do? Should I forgive him and give him another chance? Should I believe him? I mean, I would like him to be there for our baby.

I look at him and start to smile. "Okay."

"Yeah?" He asks with wide eyes and a huge grin on his face.

"Yes. I will give you another chance. But if there's anything else that I need to know about, that could possibly jeopardize yours and my future, you tell me, deal?" I tell him.

"Deal." He smiles.

"Okay then. But I'm telling you right now that this is your final chance and you'll have to earn my trust again ." I tell him.

"I promise. Even if it takes forever." He smirks at me.

"Okay then." I smirked.

"Daisy?" He asks me as he rubs the top of my hand with his thumb.

"Yes?" I reply.

"Can I touch your stomach?" He asks.

"Yes." I smile.

He then bends over and lays his head on my stomach with his arms wrapped around my waist as I begin to lightly stroke his hair with my fingers.

I hope that this can last and I hope that I'm not making a mistake. Although, he will soon realize that it wont be too easy to get back with me. So this will be really fun.

CHAPTER 20: Should I Trust Him?

ASHTON

It's been a couple of months and graduation was coming up. Although she has decided to finish school through online, I was still working at the school and had to worry about papers and everything to prepare for finals. For work, she quit since she knew there was no way she could work cause of her feet aching and back hurting.

I'm glad she chose to finish online in a way because she knew there'd be rumors and she worried about getting too stressed and hurting the baby since she was told that how she feels can affect the little one. So even though I miss seeing her in class, I can't ever wait to get home.

Things have gotten better with me and Daisy though. And every time we go to the appointments for ultrasounds, I can't help but have this amazing feeling as I see our child growing more and more between appointments inside of Daisy's stomach.

Her and I have also been cooking every night almost, well I have mostly for the past few weeks because she can't stand for too long cause of her back. So tonight since I had a lot of papers to grade, I decided to grab some food for us.

When I walked into the house though, it seemed that someone had broken in or something as I noticed the furniture along with other things were broken and scattered all over the floor.

"Baby? Daisy?!" I started calling out as I ran all over the house but never found her anywhere.

I began to panic and then my phone went off.

I didn't recognize the number though but of course still answered it.

"Hello?" I answered.

"Hello there lover boy!" A familiar female voice coos.

"Melrose? Oh god, do you know where..." I started to ask but she stopped me.

"Yes, I do know where your pathetic girlfriend is. But don't worry she's okay....for now." She says.

"What the hell is going on?!" I asked.

"You know, for a teacher, you're not as smart." She says.

"Where is she Janet?" I asked almost yelling.

"If you really want to know, I suggest you answer your door in the next few seconds." She says before hanging up.

A few seconds later, just as she told me, I hear a knock at my door.

When I answer it I am enraged even more now and try really hard to restrain myself.

"What the hell are you doing here?" I ask through clenched teeth.

"I'm here to help you get back your girl, son." My father says.

"I should have known you had something to do with this." I tell him.

"Please, can I come in?" He asks.

It takes me a while but I finally decide to let him in. After he enters, I shut the door behind him and we take a seat across from each other at the table.

"So talk. Cause I'm not sure how long I can keep my anger in check." I glare at him.

He nods as he takes in a breath and let's it out before starting to explain.

"I understand you want nothing to do with me. That's why you changed your name and distanced yourself from us." He starts.

"I don't have time to discuss our family history and issues. I just care about Daisy." I fold my hands over my chest and clench my jaw.

"I know. As far as your girlfriend goes and getting her back it's gonna take more than money." He says. Her mother's boyfriend, Roger has been working for me up until a few weeks ago. Now he's demanding money and the amount he wants is more than I have." He confesses.

"I find that hard to believe. You have more money than anyone in the world, even if it is dirty." I state.

"Yeah well, I've tried to do better. In fact, a few days after Roger left I stepped down from being the leader of the mafia and am trying to start a new life. In fact I've been talking with the FBI and explained what's going so, I have come to tell you that everything will be okay. And I know I can't take back what I've ever put you through." He says and stops himself as he's choking back tears.

I look at him a while trying to think about how he's right about what hell he put me through being the biggest mafia leader's son. That's why I escaped when I got old enough to understand what exactly he did for a living. Which reminds me.

"Where's mom?" I asked him.

"She enjoys that lifestyle too much and is a lot like Melrose so she stayed behind and we're no longer together." He states.

We both then next share an awkward moment of silence before I say anything.

"Sorry to hear that dad." I can't believe that I feel bad for him.

"Yeah well, that's not what's important right now. Right now, we need to get back your girl." He smiles at me.

"Yeah." I replied.

"So then first things first.." He states as he takes out his phone and quickly calls someone.

"Who are you calling?" I ask him thinking he's calling his old friends.

"Agent Williams? He's on board. You can come in now." He says and hangs up.

"The agents are already here?" I asked confused.

"Yep." He smirked and next thing I see is the door opening and in comes walking a bunch of FBI agents with the letters and badges showing as they enter.

"Agent Williams. Don't worry, we'll get your girl back." He shakes my hand and approaches me.

CHAPTER 21: I'm Coming For You

DAISY

I wake up in darkness and one of the things I am hit with is a foul odor coming from where this place is that I'm at.

I don't remember much but I do remember someone breaking into the house and I know by the physique of the intruder that it was a male behind the ski mask and wearing all black, including black gloves.

He had something in his hand, a white handkerchief then everything went black. Now I'm in this unkempt shack that looks worn down and am sitting on a mattress, chained to a metal pole off on the left side of me where my feet are chained together at along with my wrists zip tied together.

The door suddenly opens up and in walks two all too familiar figures who though I'm not surprised that they would be the ones behind all of this but I am a bit confused at the same time as to WHY they are doing this.

"Well look who's finally awake." Melrose greets me with a grin as does Roger who is standing next to her.

"Hey my little princess." He remarks in a vile and repulsive tone of voice that also matched the look on his face as he looked me up and down.

"Why are you doing this? I don't have any money or anything." I begin to tell them.

They both look at each other and start to laugh before looking back at me.

"No shit dumb ass." Roger says.

"Then what are you expecting?" I dared to ask.

"Your boyfriend will know what we want very soon, if he hasn't already." He smirks.

"That'a right. His father supposedly had gotten in contact with the FBI and thinks he can trick us but, his father is smarter than that. He'll give us what we want." Melrose grins.

"That's right baby." Roger grins and winks at Melrose as he wraps his arm around her waist and pulls her in closer to him as they make out.

Then suddenly a terrible idea hit me. What did they do to my mom?

"Oh and don't worry about your mom. We thought you wouldn't mind if we got rid of her for ya. Consider it as our gift to you." Melrose smirks.

Now it's true for obvious reasons as we all know that I hated my mom but not enough to where it still wouldn't hurt to hear she died. She still didn't deserve to be killed.

"You people are sick." I say with much disgust.

They both just start laughing in a menacing way at me.

"Come on baby. Let's go grab some lunch before our guests arrive." I hear her tell Roger as he loops her arm through his and they start walking off together.

Meanwhile, I start looking for something I could use to remove these shackles and zip ties.

"It's alright baby." I begin talking to my stomach. "Mommy's gonna get us out of here. Or hopefully daddy will come soon." I say worried and scared of the worst as I do not see anything I could use while I look all around.

There were a few hours that pass by and I seem to have fallen asleep somehow, probably from crying when I am woken up by the loud bang of a heavy medal door being swung opened and in walks Roger who's pulling another person by the arm who has a bag over their head and zipties around their wrists too. It looks to be a girl.

"Here, thought you could use some company." He says as he quickly removes the bag over the girls head and pushes her harshly down next to me.

I look and immediately happy yet sad at the same time to see that it's my best friend Janet.

"Janet? Oh my god." I start to tell her as I remove the gag from her mouth and see how exhausted and pale she looks and how dark her eyes are.

She opens her eyes and throws her tied up wrists over my head as I do with her and we hug each other.

"Oh Daisy thank god you're alive." She says.

Although now she looks a little more energetic and even happy?

"What did they do to you?" I ask as I look at a few scratches on her body and some dried up blood in the corner of her mouth.

"Eh. Nothing I couldn't handle." She smiles.

"Why are you smiling like that?" I asked.

"Because I'm here to help you out of here." She says.

"What?" I asked in confusion. "How the hell did you ever even get in here?" I asked.

"Well, after heading over to your man's house and noticed a bunch of FBI agents all around and after hear Ashton's plan, I had to get in on it. I've always wanted to be undercover and hopefully work for them one day and since I've been hit before and shit, I figured, why not have this be my first assignment?!" She smirks.

"Janet. This isn't a game. Roger and Melrose..." I started until she interrupted me and took out a cell phone she had put inside of her bra and handed it to me.

"What the hell?!" I whispered yelled seeing as to how I wasn't sure if rather or not Roger or any of them could hear us.

"Go ahead, dial 1 and press SEND." She says.

Then the next thing I notice is her taking a sharp tool wrapped in a handkerchief be pulled out from her underwear as she starts to undo the zip ties to her and then to me.

"How did you sneek all this in?" I asked.

"You don't want to know. But actually since those two idiots are OBVIOUSLY new at this bullshit, I had to sneek these in. Now go ahead, he's waiting." She smiles.

I press 1 then hit SEND and the other end starts ringing. Within the first ring I hear the voice I've been longing to hear.

"Hello my love. I'm coming to get you." I hear Ashton tell me.

CHAPTER 22: I'm Worried.....

ASHTON

After getting off the phone with Daisy, I felt a little more relieved to be honest and the fact that her best friend Janet volunteered to help out and purposely risk her life to get inside the place Roger and Melrose were holding Daisy captive, I was mind blown but very thankful.

My dad and I have had some time to talk but mainly focused on what was going on at the moment.

When I heard Daisy's voice, I could tell she was exhausted. It hurts me to know that out of all the shit she has gone through and then this to be added on top was unbelievable.

I had promised to help protect her and feel I have failed miserably with it because this whole thing had to do with my father.

While waiting for us to leave and head over to go and get Daisy and rescue Janet also, I was sitting on the couch just praying and hoping

I made it in time. I could never forgive myself if anything ever were to happen to her and our unborn child.

I then noticed out the corner of my eye my dad walking over towards me and taking a seat.

"How you holding up?" He asks.

"I'm just ready to go." I reply.

"I'm sorry I got you into this son. I had thought that for once I could make things right and hopefully make things better between us but, I've failed you again." My dad says.

"Yeah well..." I started but he stopped me.

"I don't expect you to ever forgive me but I do want you to know that I love you. I have since the moment I held you in my arms. And even though there's no excuse for what kind of dad I became, I hope one day you can see that I did my best with what I knew." He finishes.

I wipe quickly away a few tears and look at him.

"I never thought I'd see a day when I would say this to you but, you're gonna be a grandpa." I tell him while looking down at my hands in the my lap.

"I am?" He says with wide eyes and a big smile.

When I look at him, I smile real big in return.

"Yep. What can I say, I'm in love." I chuckle to myself a little bit.

"I'm proud of you son." He says.

"Thanks. Maybe when this is all over, we could possibly start brand new and then you can have a relationship with not just me and my girl but your grandson." I tell him.

"I'd like that." He smiles.

We next hear the lead agent for this assignment of theirs tell us to get ready and start making our way towards the car and they'll follow behind us.

I was nervous about this because I hate the idea of the person I love more than anything getting hurt on account of me.

When we did arrive in front of the rundown house that looked close to abandoned as there were a few window shutters on the outside that were halfway hanging off the sides and the unkempt dead grass and landscape surrounding the house along with overgrown weeds climbing the walls.

My dad and I made sure that our mics worked and then made our way towards the front door.

I was the person who knocked and not a moment later did Melrose open the door.

"Well finally you boys are here." She smiles. "Please come in." She smirks.

My father and I start walking inside.

"Shit! What the hell took you guys so long?!" Roger asks as he comes walking up behind her.

"Doesn't matter. We're here now!" I point out to them. "So let's get to it."

"Fine." Melrose says before she has us follow her into a very rundown and half fixed type of room.

I almost felt we were more in an abandoned shack or something as we took a seat down in the chairs and torn up dusty couch.

"So, what do you people want?" I ask.

"Well, you see, it's simple. We are wanting $500 million." Melrose states.

"What the fuck?!" My dad shouts.

"We know you have it." Roger says. "Besides, for the aggravation and inconvenience you have made this all for us, we are charging interest. Not to mention that is the price for if you want both girls back." He grins.

"What do you mean, both back?" I ask knowing who they meant.

"I swear. For a teacher you sure are stupid." Melrose insults me.

"Whatever." I roll my eyes while trying to keep myself from losing it.

Before anything else can happen, we next hear some kind of loud bang and thump come from not too far down the hallway.

"What was that?!" My dad asked.

It was quiet for a brief moment and then next thing I remember, my dad and I both quickly stand up the moment we hear a door bursting opened and out comes running Janet and Daisy hand in hand.

So my dad and I had taken that opportunity to get up and start fighting with them before they got a chance to shoot us.

"Ashton!" I hear Daisy call out to me.

"Daisy!" I shout back. "Get out of here!" I yell at her and Janet and Janet begins having her run towards the back and then a fight breaks out between all of us and I normally don't feel it's right to hit a woman but with it being Melrose, I need to make an exception.

As we're throwing punches and it seems like my dad and I are winning, we start hearing a lot of gunfire outside that has us all stop for a second and next we see both Janet and Daisy are being pushed back in by a few agents who all have a gun pointing to the girls' heads.

"What the fuck is going on?!" I asked confused.

Then I hear both Melrose and Roger as they're getting up from the ground, laughing in a sinister way.

"Did you both really think we didn't know about any of this? How else do you think these so called agents knew where to fond your father?" Roger asks as he spits blood out from his mouth.

What the fuck is going on?! Where's all the agents?!

"What about the other agents?" My father asks.

"Oh they were real. These few however, they work for me." Roger exclaims.

Oh god. This isn't good. There's only one way this can end and I can't even think about it.

CHAPTER 23: It's All Over

DAISY

Okay, now I'm confused and lost more than anything. Is there no other help?

Right now. I am starting to believe this is the end. The real agents were killed outside because Roger had these assholes pose as FBI agents just to get to my Ashton and me.

While we are all being tied up with our hands behind the chair and our ankles being tied to the chair legs, I try and think up of something that I'm not sure entirely will work but am willing to try.

I look around and see that Melrose is talking with the guy who posed to be the head of the 'fake' operation. Then I notice that Roger is on his phone leaning against the wall as a couple of guys are finishing up tying us to the chairs.

"Um, Roger?" I ask though I can't believe I'm doing this but before the guy puts the duct tape over my mouth, this is the best time to try something.

"What?!" He snaps.

"I have to pee." I tell him.

"So pee then. I'm not untying you." He states before he goes back to his phone.

Melrose and them are still in the other room and haven't heard us. I look out the corner of my eye and notice Ashton is looking at me confused. But I give him a wink so he can hopefully trust me. Then I look back at Roger.

"Please Roger! Plus, I wanted to ask you something." I plead.

"What?!" He asks frustrated.

"Not in front of everyone." I tell him while biting my lower lip a little seductively.

He looks at me questioning, I'm sure, if rather or not he should trust me or not. Which he shouldn't but hopefully he does.

He finally lets out a breath while looking me up and down and wetting his lips a little bit.

"Alright. But try anything I swear I'll kill lover boy over there." He says while nodding over towards Ashton.

"I understand." I tell him.

Janet, Ashton and his dad are all looking at me confused and giving me 'what the fuck' looks.

Once he cut the zip ties off and released my hands and then my ankles, he harshly yanked me up out of my seat and started walking me towards the bathroom when I stopped and quickly grabbed his gun that was in the back of his pants before he could and pointed it at him.

"What the fuck?!" He asks surprised.

"Untie them!" I demand.

"The fuck I will." He says.

I cocked the gun to prepare to fire.

"I said to untie them!" I demanded again. Which caught the attention of Melrose and the others who all immediately drew their guns towards me but I didn't care.

"Fucking bitch!" Melrose says. "Who the fuck untied her?!" She exclaims.

"This pervert here." I answer her while not breaking contact.

"Well I hate to tell you Sugar Cakes but, that gun ain't even loaded." Roger states.

"Really?" I asked and then shot at his knee cap. "Well look at that, it IS loaded." I stated as he dropped to his knees screaming in pain. "Something I learned and paid attention to from you was that never did you tell the truth."

"You do realize you're out numbered right?" Melrose states.

I then point the gun at her as I back away from Roger while he's still on his knees screaming in pain.

"I don't care. I will pull this trigger before those dumbasses do." I call her bluff just like I did with Roger. "Now untie them." I ask again.

She looks at me a moment longer and then she motions with her head to the guy behind us to do it.

I never take my eyes off of her or the guys beside her and I hear the tape ripping off their mouths and next hear a loud punching sound and when I quickly turn to look, I see Ashton beating the hell out of that guy while grabbing his gun and the next thing I know we are all getting into a big brawl as Melrose knocks the gun out of my hand and punches me and we then start going at it with each other.

"He was mine and your fat ugly ass took him away from him!" She yells at me.

"He wanted to be with a woman not a dirty slut that he'd catch a disease from!" I yelled back while kicking her off of me.

We begin throwing more and more punches at each other and can't keep track of Janet or anyone.

To be honest I am surprised at how strong I am and thankful too for that and still being mindful of being careful the baby doesn't get hit.

Between the firing of the guns and the screams, yells as well as fighting and breaking of furniture, I next felt something heavy hit me from behind, knocking me onto the ground.

As soon as I turn around and see Melrose pointing a gun at me, I next see Ashton come up behind her and grab her and try to fight with her to take the gun out from her hand.

He finally is able to and punches her hard onto the ground, knocking her out and runs to my side making sure I'm okay.

Thank god that the next sounds we hear are police sirens.

'It's okay baby. Everything is going to be okay." He assures me.

EPILOGUE: Five Years Later

DAISY

Once the rest of the REAL authorities came literally just in time, they took Melrose away and never charged any of us including Ashton's dad with the couple of people they ended up shooting and killing in self defense of course.

Ashton's dead had been put into a Witness Protection Program and then given a different name and whole identity and though he was able to stay in contact with us, he also was paranoid and thought it'd be best that he moved away and started anew somewhere and check in on us occasionally.In which he kept his promise.

The moment that Janet finished high school, she right away went off to become an FBI Agent and now is one of their youngest and top agents in charge of operations for going undercover in the human trafficking. She has helped capture a lot of people and still is doing great.

Me and Ashton had gotten married a few months after I graduated high school and we had our son.

Then today happens to be our son's fifth birthday and Janet brought over her three year old and husband as we all had the party at a beach.

We were having fun playing in the water hanging out and were enjoying ourselves when I heard my little man laughing really hard nearby from the water, I had noticed he was sitting on Ashton's shoulders and was holding onto our son's feet while he held onto Ashton's head.

"That was fun dad!" He shouted while laughing.

"Good. We'll go back and do it later cause we gotta get something to eat buddy." Ashton tells him.

"I want a burger!" He shouts out!

"Alright." Ashton laughs.

He brings him closer and starts making his plate before sitting him down with his friends on a big beach blanket and next comes walking up behind me while I was talking with Janet and them and he scoops me up bridal style right before then carrying me over towards the water.

"Baby!" I scream. "I don't want to go in the water." I tell him.

He continues walking towards there laughing.

"Well you need to get in some time." He laughs.

"Put me down! But not in the water or I'll bring you down with me!" I warn him and he continues walking into the water before then dunking both of us in.

~~~~~~~~~~~~

ASHTON

The moment we got up from the water, she wiped her eyes and I couldn't help but laugh at her.

She then splashed and stood up with small waves hitting us.

"You jerk!" She pushes me and I just laugh before I pick her up again and carry her back out of the water and put her onto the sand again after she began moving her legs and kicking to get down.

"That's enough of that!" I tell her and throw her over my shoulder as I smack her ass and she yelps and then smacks mine and then finally laughs.

When we get back to everybody, we both give each other a kiss and go back to hanging out with everyone.

When the sun was setting, me and her walked hand in hand along the sand by the water and then stopped to look at the sunset while our son was back with Janet and her husband by the fire they had just made.
~~~~~~~~~~~~

Me and Daisy face the sunset and I stand behind her and have my arms wrapped around her waist while placing my chin on her shoulder.

"I love you." I tell her.

"I love you too." She tells me.

I never thought I would ever find somebody like her and never thought I would ever have a relationship with my dad ever again but I do now. And I owe all the good in my life to her.

What can I say, I fell in love with my FAVORITE student!

CPSIA information can be obtained
at www.ICGtesting.com
Printed in the USA
LVHW081253101122
732762LV00014B/918